TOM PERCIVAL

Danny
AND THE
Slippery
Stress

A fantastic **DREAM DEFENDERS** adventure!

First published 2022 by Macmillan Children's Books
an imprint of Pan Macmillan
The Smithson, 6 Briset Street, London EC1M 5NR
EU representative: Macmillan Publishers Ireland Ltd, 1st Floor,
The Liffey Trust Centre, 117–126 Sheriff Street Upper
Dublin 1, D01 YC43
Associated companies throughout the world
www.panmacmillan.com

ISBN 978-1-5290-2921-5

1 3 5 7 9 8 6 4 2

A CIP catalogue record for this book is available from the British Library.

Printed and bound by CPI Group (UK) Ltd, Croydon CR0 4YY

With thanks to Holmen Paper, Gould Paper Sales
and CPI Books for their support.

This book is dedicated to Ollie Todd-Archer!

So Ollie, this is YOUR book, but only in a manner of speaking. If you happen to see someone else reading this book, it doesn't mean that you can snatch it off them and say 'This is my book!', okay?

There, I hope that's all clear now.
Best wishes, Tom.

CHAPTER
1

Erika Delgano yawned as she woke up. The sun was shining in through the open window, warming her face. She smiled lazily and opened her eyes.

'How *nice* of you to come back to us, Erika!' said Mr Jolly from the front of the class. His jaw was clenched and his bushy eyebrows were dipping into a furious, hairy collision just above his nose. 'I'm terribly sorry that you seem to find my lessons SO boring that

you actually fall asleep! I don't suppose you have an answer to my question, do you?'

Erika jolted upright, trying to remember the last thing she'd heard. Her best friend Kris was gesturing wildly at her, his hands dancing around in the air. What was he trying to say? 'Er . . . the great fire of London?' said Erika, doubtfully.

'We're in a maths lesson, Erika!' exploded her teacher.

Mr Jolly's name was misleading. He was never particularly jolly at the best of times, but right now he was *exceptionally* un-jolly. 'Report to the library for detention at lunchtime and please try to stay awake in lessons in the future!'

Erika tried her best to look sad and upset, but really? Detention in the library? That was **FUN!** It was like being given detention in a sweet shop.

'How come you fell asleep, Erika?' asked Kris after the lesson had finished. 'I mean, I know that Mr Jolly can go on a bit, but all the same!'

Erika frowned. This bit was always hard. She hated keeping secrets from her best friend, but she couldn't tell *anyone* what she got up to at night. She was a member of the **TOP-SECRET DREAM DEFENDERS** – it was their job to keep everyone dreaming happily, and as a key member of the team, Erika's nights could get kind of busy.

Last night she'd been involved in an especially tricky case where they'd been chasing a rogue Nightmare across several different dreams, and, if anything, she'd woken up more tired than when she'd gone to bed.

But she couldn't tell Kris any of that.

'Randall was sick in the night,' she said as they walked onto the school yard. Erika's little brother was only a toddler. She felt bad about lying, but what other option did she have?

'Is he feeling better now?' asked Kris.

'Yeah, he's fine, thanks,' said Erika, keen to end the conversation.

'DUCK!' shouted a voice suddenly.

Erika moved with the reactions of a tiger, swiftly crouching to the floor as a football shot over her head.

Kris moved with the reactions of a stuffed goldfish. He turned to face whoever had shouted **'DUCK'**.

'Wh—' he started to say. And then a
football hit him straight in the face.

Kris's glasses flew off and he dropped his
bag, spilling pencils and books everywhere.
A few kids started laughing until a clear,
confident voice called out, 'Hey! Cut that
out! How would *you* like it?'

It was Danny Forsyth, a boy from the top year. He strode over and bent down to pick up Kris's glasses.

'Are you OK?' asked Danny.

Kris nodded, but he was unsteady on his feet and his eyes were swimming.

'Someone pick up his stuff,' called

Danny. Several children scrambled over, all keen to help.

Danny put his arm round Kris's shoulder and led him over to a bench. 'Sorry about that,' he said. 'I've been helping some of the younger kids with their penalties. They're getting the hang of the power, but it looks like we need to work on accuracy!' He smiled apologetically.

Danny Forsyth was the undisputed STAR of the school. He played on ALL the school teams and was captain of most of them too. He was the founder of the school chess club *and* its debating team, and he coached the kids in the younger years with their netball and football.

Basically, everybody liked Danny Forsyth.

Kris stared at him in awe.

'Feeling a bit better?' asked Danny.

'Bluuuuuugh . . .' mumbled Kris.

Erika suspected this was not so much because his head hurt, but because he didn't know what to say.

'It'll probably sting for a bit,' said Danny, clapping Kris on the back. 'I'd better crack on. It's the big match against Swinnerton's School this afternoon, and I need to get some practice in! See you later, Craig!' Then he sprang up from the bench and was gone.

'He knows my name!' said Kris in a soft voice.

'Er, no he doesn't,' said Erika. 'He

just called you Craig.'

Kris scowled at her. 'Well, it's close enough!'

Erika shook her head. 'Anyway, I'd better go to my detention. See you after school?'

'Yeah, see you later, Erika!' said Kris, taking his neatly packed bag from a girl who looked very disappointed to see that Danny had already left.

Erika was just about to walk into the library when her necklace buzzed three times. It was a message from the **DREAM DEFENDERS!** Spinning on her heel, she changed direction and crept round the back of the library. None of the students were meant to go here, but a message from the **DREAM DEFENDERS** was

important. She couldn't risk anyone else hearing it. When she was sure she was completely alone, she took out the crystal on the necklace and tapped it. A beam shot out, creating a hologram of a giraffe in front of her.

'Is it recording?' said the giraffe.

'I dunno,' grunted a deep voice from somewhere off screen. 'I'm not tech support, am I?'

Erika smiled. Her friends in the **DREAM DEFENDERS** were certainly . . . *unusual*.

'Urghhh! I hate recording messages,' said the giraffe. It looked down and stroked its very long neck with one hoof. 'Whoops! Sorry, Erika. I hadn't realized! Give me a second, I'll just get changed!'

In a fluid, blurry motion, the giraffe somehow became a girl about Erika's age. Even though Erika had seen her friend Sim shapeshift more times than she could count, it was still totally bizarre to see it happening.

'Guess what?' continued Sim. 'We're

helping someone from your school tonight! Pretty cool, right? It would be good if you can get as much information as—' The hologram flickered, and all Erika could see was Sim, frozen in place. Then the image stuttered, played through on fast forward for a few seconds and finally went back to normal.

'Sorry! We're having a few technical issues!' said Sim.

'**LOTS** of technical issues,' muttered the gravelly voice off camera. 'No surprise though, is it? Those boffins messing it up at their desks, while we're out here risking life and limb!'

That was Wade, one of the older members of the **DREAM DEFENDERS**. Wade was very skilled and highly experienced, but he could sometimes be a *teeny*, *tiny*, *little* bit **TOTALLY MISERABLE**.

'OK! *OK!* Calm down, Wade!' said Sim. 'Now, Erika, the person whose dream we're going into is—' Again the hologram glitched, and all Erika could make out was, 'Ah—zn—ki—ta—ta—ta—ta—cha.'

Then the projection flickered back into life again, and Sim's recording started playing normally. 'So keep an eye out for any strange behaviour that might help us tonight and—'

There was a grinding buzz and the hologram completely vanished.

Erika scratched her head – someone from her school needed the Dream

14

Defenders' help? But *who*? She mulled it over as she walked back round the side of the library. There were **LOTS** of kids who could do with a bit of hand in school. What if it was Kris?

Erika nodded thoughtfully. It was almost certainly Kris. He'd recently developed a fear of pencil cases to go along with his fear of baked beans. One of the boys in their class had recently got a pencil case that looked like a tin of baked beans, which was causing **ALL SORTS** of problems.

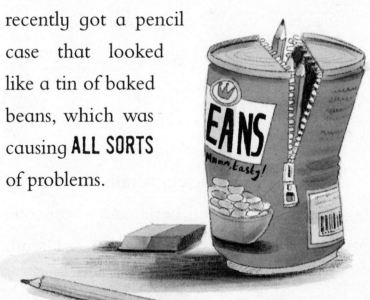

Just as Erika crept back out from the side of the library, she saw Mr Jolly. He was glaring at her. Her shoulders slumped as Mr Jolly's furry eyebrows waggled at her.

'Hanging around in banned locations?' he barked. 'We'd better make that *two* detentions, don't you think, Erika?'

'Yes, sir,' Erika sighed. 'Sorry, sir.'

CHAPTER
2

Later that night, Erika was outside, gazing upwards. The moon was low in the sky, swaying slightly from side to side because it was hanging from a bit of old string. A flock of miniature badgers flew past, humming famous pop songs as they sprinkled rainbow-coloured fairy dust all around the enormous clock face that Erika was standing on.

Erika frowned and glanced at her watch. She shouldn't even be in this dream. She should have automatically arrived at **DREAM DEFENDERS HQ** as soon as she'd fallen asleep. What had gone wrong?

She thought back over what had just happened. It had been a completely ordinary evening full of what she liked to call TUFS (Totally Usual Family Stuff).

She'd watched TV with her parents while Randall repeatedly bashed one of his toys against the floor. Eventually, Erika's mum had lost her patience and taken the toy away. This had stopped the banging noise, but immediately started a brand-new, even more annoying, super-loud-crying noise.

Erika had slipped upstairs to read her book – with her headphones on. Then, when everything had gone quiet, she'd

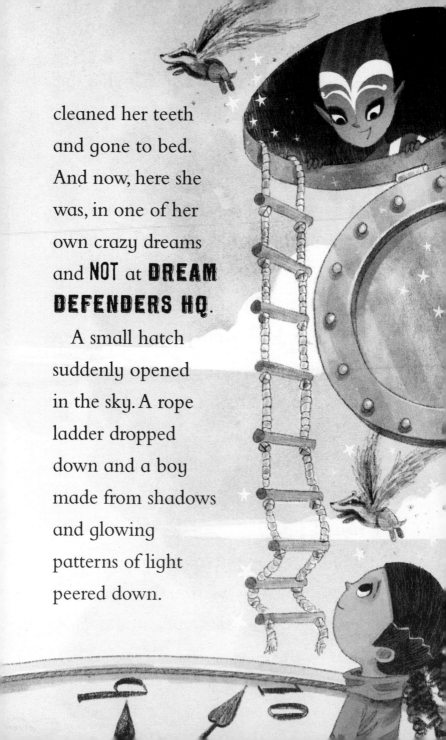

cleaned her teeth and gone to bed. And now, here she was, in one of her own crazy dreams and **NOT** at **DREAM DEFENDERS HQ**.

A small hatch suddenly opened in the sky. A rope ladder dropped down and a boy made from shadows and glowing patterns of light peered down.

'Silas!' called Erika. 'What's going on? How come I'm not at HQ?'

'Technical issues!' called Silas. 'Something's a bit screwy with all our systems right now, so we're doing this the old-fashioned way! Come on up, I'll explain.'

'OK,' replied Erika, climbing up the rope ladder. Each time she took her foot off a rung, it evaporated in a puff of smoke. It looked really cool, but it was a bit disconcerting.

She eventually pulled herself up through the hatch in the sky and closed it firmly shut behind her. She stood in a small, drab maintenance tunnel that looked a world away from the wonderful dream she'd just been in. A loud yell of,

'**Heebie Jeebie!**' rang out and Erika was almost knocked off her feet by a small, furry cannonball that shot towards her and clung on to her legs.

'Hey, Beastling!' said Erika, grinning as she tickled the cannonball's ears.

Beastling hugged Erika tightly and whispered, '**Heebie Jeebie**,' again. A speech bubble appeared in the air showing a picture of a happy face, two letter 'C's and a letter 'U'.

'I'm happy to see you too, buddy!' replied Erika, patting him on his small, furry back.

Beastling only ever spoke in pictures, which looked amazing but could be slightly challenging at times.

'You would not *believe* the night we've had!' exclaimed Silas, prying Beastling off Erika's legs. 'Seriously, anything that could go wrong, *did* go wrong! Most of our comms are down; transportation's down. The whole lot! Anyway, come on, let's get back to HQ!'

Silas held out his hands towards Erika and Beastling, who each took one. 'Ready?' he asked. Silas had several unique abilities, but by far the most impressive was teleportation. Before Erika had even finished nodding, they were all standing in the circular briefing room back at **DREAM DEFENDERS HQ**.

Wade and Sim were already sitting around the large table in the middle of the room. Their unit commander, Madam Hettyforth, was standing next to an old-fashioned projector, fiddling with the controls and muttering under her breath.

'Ah, Erika!' said Madam Hettyforth, looking over with a smile. 'You made it!

Sorry it's all been a bit of a performance. I don't know what the woolly-word is going on with our systems. Still, at least you're here now. Were you able to find anything out about our subject while you were in school?'

Erika shook her head. 'The message was glitching, so I couldn't hear who the subject was. I have a good idea who it *might* be though.'

'Oh well.' Madam Hettyforth sighed. 'It doesn't really matter; we'll just have to start from scratch. So, the child we're helping tonight is . . .' She paused to look down at her notes.

'Kris Holmes?' suggested Erika.

'Your friend Kris?' said Madam Hettyforth, looking confused. 'Goodness me, no! No, this is a young chap called . . .' She scoured the folder of notes again. 'Danny Forsyth.'

Erika blinked. 'Sorry, what?' she asked. 'Do you mean *THE* Danny Forsyth?'

Madam Hettyforth checked her notes again. 'That's correct. Danny Forsyth. Why?'

Erika shook her head. 'Well, it's just that he's . . . Well, he's pretty much amazing! Clever, sporty, popular, and really nice too! How could *he* need our help?'

'You shouldn't jump to conclusions, Erika,' grumbled Wade. 'You know, look at me. Now, I know that sometimes, on the outside, I can seem a bit grumpy, miserable or irritable. But actually, what's happening is that deep down, on the inside —' he paused, meaningfully — 'I'm usually hungry. And it's that hungry feeling which makes me *seem* grumpy. Do you see what I mean?'

'Er, sorry to interrupt, Wade,' said Silas. 'But the way that you seem is exactly the way that you are. Being hungry is just your *reason* for feeling grumpy.'

Wade's stony face darkened. He frowned with an alarmingly loud, grinding sound. 'The details aren't important!' he growled. 'You know what I mean. Basically, we shouldn't jump to conclusions until we know a bit more about him. Right, Ma'am?'

Madam Hettyforth nodded. 'Wade's quite right. Now, I was going to try to show you some clips of Danny's life on this projector, but even that's stopped working, so you're just going to have to jump straight into his dream and see what you can find out.' She looked round at the group sternly. 'Tonight is a fact-finding mission only. After all, we can't help him solve his problems until we know what they are. So, stay hidden and let's just try to work out what's going on here. Then we'll patch it all up tomorrow night. All clear?'

Everyone nodded. They headed down to the vast chamber at the centre of **DREAM DEFENDERS HQ**. It was filled with countless rows of portals, each one leading into a different dream. Silas led the way to Danny's portal.

'OK!' said Silas, keying in the activation code. 'Here we go!'

CHAPTER 3

'So far, so weird!' murmured Sim as they arrived in the middle of an enormous football stadium. The tiered rows of seating rose impossibly high above Erika's head, each one packed with spectators all chanting and cheering Danny's name. It was so huge that there were even stars and clouds drifting across *inside* the stadium.

On the pitch in front of them, Danny was preparing to take a penalty. Unfortunately for him, the goalkeeper was an elephant that filled almost the

entire goal. Danny's brow was furrowed in concentration. He looked at the goalposts. He looked at the ball. He looked at the goalie. He looked back at the ball. Deafening cheers echoed around the stadium.

Danny suddenly narrowed his eyes in concentration and ran towards the ball.

SMACK!

The ball arced through the air, curling straight towards the top-left corner of the goal – the only clear space. The elephant tried to reach his trunk up, but was too slow.

The crowd went **WILD**. Everyone was dancing and singing – apart from Danny. He just clenched his fists tight, shut his eyes and nodded slightly.

'What's that all about?' whispered Erika. 'If I'd just scored a goal like that, I'd be bouncing off the ceiling!'

'Yeah, it wasn't a *bad* shot, either,' muttered Wade. 'Although, I'd have probably gone top right. I've always been pretty good at football.'

Beastling looked at Wade, raised one eyebrow and made a speech bubble with a picture of Pinocchio's nose growing longer and longer.

'You watch it, *furball!*' growled Wade.

All of a sudden, the dream changed. The stadium melted away and Danny, Erika and the rest of **DREAM DEFENDERS** were now standing on a narrow, rickety bridge, over an impossibly wide ravine. Erika peered over the edge, but she couldn't make out anything below her. The ravine seemed to drop down forever. She kicked a small stone off the bridge and waited, but no sound came.

'We're pretty high up!' she whispered.

'No need to whisper,' replied Silas, waving his hands right in front of Danny's face. 'He can't see us or hear us. It's like we're not even here.'

'Oh yeah!' said Erika. 'I forgot!'

Danny set off across the bridge with brisk, confident steps. But as he walked, sections of the bridge dislodged themselves, dropping into the void, leaving big gaps in the bridge. Danny frowned. The further he went, the more of it vanished. But when he turned around or walked backwards, the bridge in front of him rebuilt itself.

'It looks to me like his subconscious is making problems for him,' murmured Silas thoughtfully.

Danny stopped in front of a particularly large gap. He took a few steps back and tried taking a run-up, but by the time he reached the edge it was impossibly wide. He stopped running just in time, grabbing hold of the handrail to stop himself plunging into the nothingness. Breathing deeply, Danny scratched his

chin and squinted out at the bridge, his eyebrows knitting together in a frown.

'Shall we try to help?' asked Erika

'Ma'am said this was just a fact-finding mission,' Wade reminded her. 'We're just trying to get information right now.'

'I suppose . . .' said Erika, shaking her head. 'It's hard though, isn't it? Watching someone struggle like this, I mean – *Wait!* What's that?' Erika squinted.

Far away in the distance was a swirling sinuous shape, twisting through the air. Erika grabbed a set of binoculars from Wade. In more detail, the creature looked even more unsettling. It bubbled and boiled, stuttering and jerking like old-fashioned film footage, constantly changing and shifting into a different

shape. She
passed the
binoculars to Sim,
who took a look and gasped.

'Any ideas what we do now?' asked
Erika, backing warily away.

'This is a reconnaissance mission,'
repeated Wade. 'We need to just—'

'I *know* it's a reconnaissance mission!'
interrupted Erika. 'But whatever that

thing is, it's getting closer, and I don't think that it's coming to offer Danny an ice cream! We need to do something!'

Wade sighed heavily. 'I suppose that we *could* give him a bit of a helping hand. If he died while we were on duty, the paperwork would be horrendous!'

'I'm on it!' yelled Sim. 'I'll deactivate my cloaking, give me a second—'

The air rippled around Sim and then she morphed into a huge floating hand with wings on either side. She swept through the air past the rest of the **DREAM DEFENDERS** to hover in front of the broken end of the bridge just in front of Danny.

'I didn't mean a *literal* helping hand!' shouted Wade. 'You could have just made yourself look like more of the bridge!'

Sim laughed. 'And where's the fun in that?'

'Whaaaaaat!' Danny had just noticed the giant flying hand in front of him. 'Where's the fun in what? Actually, *wait*!' He blinked as his brain tried to make sense of what it was seeing. 'What *are* you?'

'Well, currently, I'm a giant floating hand with wings,' replied Sim. 'Now look, I don't want to alarm you, but racing up behind you is a massive unidentified potentially lethal creature.'

Danny spun around in alarm, but then he frowned. 'There's nothing there!' he protested.

'There most definitely is!' replied Sim.

'*Surely* you can see it? Sort of horrific-looking? A vague suggestion of a hideous slathering mouth? Far too many teeth? Lots of claws? And it's getting closer, VERY quickly.'

Danny squinted. 'But *where*? I can't see anything!'

The monster roared as it sped towards them and out shot a fetid blast of stinking breath. Erika's ears rang as the ground trembled beneath her feet. *What was that thing*? She peered over her shoulder. Whatever it was, it was getting closer by the second and they were all trapped on this rickety old bridge, stuck behind Danny.

'We don't have time for this!' hissed Silas, shaking his head. 'Wade, do the

Full Awareness Blast!'

Wade nodded, pulled out a strange-looking device with a torch on one end of it and fired off a flash of dazzling brightness.

As the F.A.B. took effect, Danny's eyes widened. Wordlessly, he looked between Silas, Wade and Beastling, staring open-mouthed.

'OK, so don't panic!' said Erika in what she hoped was a soothing voice – but it was very hard to sound soothing when your nerves were jangling like alarm bells. She took a deep breath and carried on. 'I know this is all very weird, but you need to do what we say and get out of here before that thing arrives!'

'What *thing*!' cried Danny, looking

around in all directions apart from directly at the massive creature that was now only metres away. His eyes narrowed as he looked at Erika.

'Wait,' he murmured, 'don't I know you from somewhere?'

'Yes,' Erika replied, 'from school!' She shoved Danny onto the floating hand in front of him. 'Now go! Sim, you get him to safety; we'll hold it off as long as we can!'

'Roger!' replied Sim. She beat the wings on either side of the giant hand, rising up into the air just as a giant clawed hand slashed down towards where Danny had been standing.

Erika
dived out
of the way,
landing hard.
'I told you it wasn't
bringing ice cream!' she
gasped as she scrambled up. 'We need to
get off this bridge; we're not safe here!'

'Agreed!' replied Silas. He started
sprinting, until he was just a dazzling
blur, shooting up and down the bridge.

'I'll distract it; you lot get off the bridge!'

Silas sped up even more, leaving a blinding trail of light behind him in the air. The monster reached out towards him and then roared, holding its hands up in front of its eyes.

'Now!' shouted Silas. 'Run!'

Erika covered her eyes against the dazzling light and tore towards the cliff

edge with Beastling
and Wade alongside her. But their
advantage didn't last for long. The
monster shifted into a new shape with
thick eyelids that protected it against the
dazzling flare.

'Oh . . .' muttered Silas. 'Looks like
we're going to need another plan!' He

sped through the monster's legs as it spun around, chasing them all back across the bridge to the edge of the chasm.

Erika ducked under another tentacle as it sliced towards her and dived back onto solid ground.

'Any ideas what we do now?'

'So far my plan is basically, *try not to die*,' replied Silas, teleporting out of the way as the creature flung a giant boulder at him. 'But that's just a work in progress. I'll come up with something better later!'

'No rush,' gasped Erika, as a sinuous tentacle snaked out and wrapped around her neck. 'But a better plan right *now* would be good!'

CHAPTER 4

Wade flung a rock through the air towards the tentacle that was tightening around Erika. But although the tentacle had a very real grip on Erika's neck, the rock somehow passed straight through it.

'Try something else . . .' croaked Erika as the creature's grip tightened.

Beastling leaped out of hiding, pulled a rude face at the monster and then waggled his furry bum towards it.

'Not quite what I had in mind,' wheezed Erika.

The monster shifted shape continuously – it never held any one for longer than a couple of seconds – but whatever appearance it took on, it was always jagged, harsh and malevolent. Its boiling, flickering eyes narrowed as it glared at Beastling, then swept him aside with a casual wave of one clawed hand. Silas sped forward, a dazzling blur of light and shadow moving almost too fast to be seen. Grabbing hold of Erika, he teleported them both a few metres away.

'Thanks!' gasped Erika, rubbing her neck as the monster shrieked and roared in frustration.

Wade pressed his hands to the ground, gritted his teeth and sent energy waves pouring down into the bedrock. Almost immediately, towering pillars of stone rushed skyward, closing in around the monster like a cage. Silas sped over to help at a supersonic speed. He raced around the rock cage, leaving a trail of light that solidified into a glowing rope that bound the creature.

'What now?' asked Erika, her breath slowly coming back.

'Now we—' began Wade. But even as he spoke, the monster bellowed with rage,

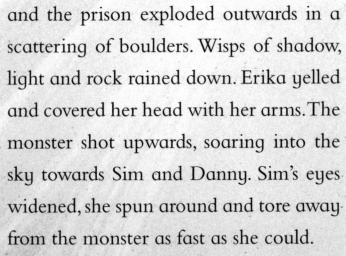

and the prison exploded outwards in a scattering of boulders. Wisps of shadow, light and rock rained down. Erika yelled and covered her head with her arms. The monster shot upwards, soaring into the sky towards Sim and Danny. Sim's eyes widened, she spun around and tore away from the monster as fast as she could.

'It can FLY?' gasped Silas. 'That's cheating!'

Twin rocket boosters suddenly appeared on the back of the giant floating hand. 'Hold on tight!' Sim yelled to Danny as the rockets activated and the hand shot forward. Blazing a trail across the sky, the giant hand shot away from the Nightmare. Down on the ground, Erika whooped and jumped in the air.

But the sound immediately died in her throat. The monster had narrowed its eyes and twisted and curled through the air, somehow following the exact course that Sim was taking. Every dip, shimmy and sudden change of direction was mirrored by the monster. It roared and screamed and shrieked as it shot after them. Second by second, it got closer.

'What are you doing!' yelled Danny. 'There's nothing there! Can't we just slow down?'

A tentacle-arm-appendage-*thing* shot out from the Nightmare and struck Sim, knocking the hand sideways. Danny stumbled and almost lost his grip. 'Watch where you're flying!' he shouted. 'I nearly fell off then – are you *trying* to kill me?'

Sim gritted her teeth and dived towards the ground. Danny gripped on tight to the giant fingers, squinting into the wind that rushed past them. The monster gave an ear-splitting howl and followed her, intent on its target. Just as Sim was about to crash into the ground, she levelled off and shot across the desert floor. Behind them, the monster was fractionally too slow. It barrelled into the ground, collapsing in a flickering, smoking heap.

Again Erika cheered. And again, she regretted it almost instantly. An impossibly long arm shot out of the monster and grabbed hold of Danny, plucking him off the giant hand easily.

'No!' Sim gasped. The monster was holding Danny up, high above its body, with an evil smile playing round its ferocious mouth. Danny's arms and legs were hanging limp, his eyes suddenly blank and vacant.

Erika looked on in horror. 'It's . . . it's like it's feeding off him somehow,' she muttered to herself.

'Sim! Over here!' yelled Silas, racing forward.

Sim banked round and sped towards Silas, who jumped onto the hand.

'Now, get me up towards Danny!' said Silas urgently. As soon as they were level with Danny, Silas leaped off the hand and grabbed hold of him. He teleported them back to the ground.

The monster blinked, and slowly shook its head. Erika thought it looked confused, but then it rubbed its belly and yawned.

'It's like it's just had a big meal!' she cried. 'Look, it's all sleepy!'

'Now's our chance!' replied Wade. 'Let's get out of here and find Silas, Sim and Danny!'

They hadn't gone far. Sim had changed back to her normal form and was standing by Silas. They were both looking at Danny, who was lying on the floor, eyes shut and ashen-faced. In the distance the monster's eyelids flickered as it slumped contentedly down on the ground.

'How long have we got?' asked Erika.

Wade shrugged. 'No idea, but I wouldn't plan a picnic here any time soon!'

'Agreed!' said Erika. Then she turned to Silas. 'Is Danny OK?' she asked. 'What happened?'

Silas shook his head. 'I'm not sure, on either count. Look, do you see his face? It's like . . . like the colour's faded out of it.'

'Well, yeah! I think I'd be looking a bit pale if that had just happened to me,' replied Erika.

Silas caught her eye. 'I don't mean like that. Look, the colour has *literally* faded out of him – like he's covered in grey dust!'

Erika peered closer at Danny – Silas was right. With a sudden gasp, Danny's eyes shot open and he sat up, the colour rushing back into his face.

'Where am I?' he blurted out. 'What's going on? What *happened*?'

'Shhh, you're OK!' said Erika, patting him on the shoulder. 'That Nightmare had you for a moment. It was holding you and it . . . Well, I don't exactly know what it did!'

Danny frowned. He seemed to have recovered quickly from whatever the Nightmare had done. 'I wish you'd all stop talking about this "monster",' said Danny, making exaggerated air quotes. 'Look, I just fell off that weird hand thing because it was flying too quickly! I must have fallen and bumped my head. I'll be *fine*!'

'But that's not what happened!' exclaimed Erika. 'There *was* a monster chasing after you, but for some reason, you couldn't see it.' She frowned. 'Do you have anything that might be bothering you? Maybe even something that you're not really aware of?'

'I'm not trying to be funny,' said Danny, 'but how could I know about something that was bothering me, if I'm not aware of it?'

'Fair point!' said Erika. 'But there's obviously something going on here. Mysterious, never-seen-before dream invaders don't just show up for no reason! What we need to do is work out why that thing appeared and *then* we can work out how to get rid of it.'

'Makes sense. You know, you should join the debating team at school.' Danny nodded thoughtfully. 'But even so, I have no idea what this "dream invader" is.'

'You really can't see that thing, like, *at all*?' asked Erika. 'You can't hear or smell it?' She wrinkled her nose. 'Because *I* certainly can.' Her eyes widened. 'Actually, I *really* can. Can anyone else smell it?'

Sim sniffed deeply and nodded, just before the ground beneath them exploded upwards. The Nightmare shot out of the ground and up into the air, scattering all the members of the **DREAM DEFENDERS** in different directions.

'What are you *doing*?' demanded Danny. 'Why are you all jumping around like that?'

'There's no way we can defeat

that monster like this!' shouted Erika, scrambling out of the way as a monstrous foot slammed down on the ground where she had just been sprawled. 'Nothing seems to be working, and if Danny can't see that thing, he's way too vulnerable. We need to get him out of here!'

'We could shut down the dream?' called Silas, darting out of the way of four tentacles. 'Danny would just wake up and you'd just get pulled back to your own dream. The monster would be trapped in here until tomorrow night. HQ won't like it though.'

'We've no choice!' yelled Erika.

Danny stood oblivious to everything, looking at Erika and the **DREAM DEFENDERS** with a puzzled expression

while the monster rose up behind him, clawed hands reaching out, a flickering tongue scratching around its cracked lips.

'Now, Silas! *Do it!*' shouted Erika.

Silas nodded. He reached into thin air and somehow pulled open a small hatch, revealing a lever with the words **EMERGENCY SHUTDOWN** written above it. 'Brace yourselves!' he shouted, grabbing hold of the handle and heaving it downward.

The last thing Erika saw as the world disintegrated into nothing was Danny's face looking at her as though she had completely lost her mind.

CHAPTER 5

Erika's eyes shot open and she peered at her alarm clock. It was six in the morning and she was back in her own bedroom, her heart still pounding after the adrenaline rush of the battle with the monster in Danny's dream.

What had happened back there? Why couldn't Danny even see the creature? Erika shook her head. All she had was questions, but the answers seemed to be harder to find. Still, at least she could try to find out some more about Danny's general life while they were at school. Maybe she'd be able to find something out that might help, some reason why that monster was after him. Erika sighed. There was nothing she could do about it at the moment though. Turning on her bedside light, Erika picked up a book and started reading. After about half an hour, she heard Randall start yelling, **'Wayyy-CUPTIME!'** over and over again.

Not long afterwards, she heard a groan from her parents' room. Randall had decided to carry on yelling, **'Wayyy-CUPTIME!'** even after everyone was clearly awake, trying to eat their breakfast and get ready for the day ahead. Erika noticed her parents looking increasingly frayed and decided to head to school early.

Despite the strangeness of the night before, the morning went pretty much as per usual. Mr Jolly was in a very bad mood. He started yelling at Anish Kureshi because he hadn't done his homework. When Susie Jenkins said that she hadn't done it either, Mr Jolly started to completely lose it. Then it turned out that *nobody* had done the homework because Mr Jolly had forgotten to set any. That put him in an even *worse* mood because he had no one to shout at, so he decided to just glare at everyone, all morning. Erika was very relieved when the bell rang.

'Coming to get some lunch?' asked

Kris as they bustled out into the corridor.

'Maybe later,' replied Erika. 'I've got something else that I need to do first.'

Kris swung his bag up over his shoulder. 'See you later then.'

Erika walked towards the end of the corridor where the year six classroom was. She didn't have long to wait – the door soon burst open and out poured a stream of children. Striding confidently along with them all was Danny Forsyth.

It felt surreal to see Danny there in ordinary, normal, everyday life, when just a few hours ago she'd been talking with him on the edge of an impossibly tall cliff next to a magical bridge. Erika almost called out to him, before realizing that he wouldn't remember any of what had happened in the Dreamscape and would have no idea who she was.

Erika needed a way to get to speak to him. *But how?*

An idea suddenly occurred to her. She didn't like it much, and it was going to be embarrassing, but there was no time to waste. Erika stepped forward just as Danny was approaching and suddenly stopped, pretending to fumble around in her bag.

There was a crash as Danny collided with her, and the two of them were sent tumbling to the floor.

'Sorry about that!' gasped Danny, springing to his feet. Erika groaned. She'd landed heavily and her elbow hurt. 'Are you hurt?' Danny asked, helping her up.

'I'm fine,'
muttered Erika,
wincing at the burning
pain around her elbow.

Danny looked at her, and his
eyes narrowed.

'Wait . . .' he murmured. 'Don't I know
you from somewhere?'

Erika grinned. 'Well, yeah! We do go
to the same school, you know.'

'I guess . . .' said Danny, but he didn't sound convinced.

'You were helping my friend yesterday,' said Erika quickly. 'He'd just been hit in the face with a football.'

'Ah, right. I remember now.' Danny nodded. 'So, what's your name?'

'Erika.'

Danny handed Erika her bag. 'Well, like I said, sorry about that, but I'd better be off now. There's a big hockey match this week, and we've got practice now.'

'It's funny you say that!' blurted Erika. 'I was going to try out for the hockey team.' She paused and then added, 'I'm really good at catching and throwing!'

'*Right.*' Danny frowned at her. 'It's just that I've never seen you at hockey club.'

'No,' said Erika, 'I've never been. All the same, you should see me smack that ball in the hoop!' She mimed swinging a bat through the air. '*Boom!*'

There was a brief pause.

'Have you ever actually played hockey before?' asked Danny.

'Well, no, I've not *played* it as such,' said Erika. 'But I'm fairly sure I could spell it! Look, I just want to give it a shot. Do you mind if I tag along?'

'OK,' said Danny, shrugging. 'Come on, you can help me get all the kit out.'

Danny's friends in the hockey club looked surprised to see Erika strolling along casually beside him, but not as surprised as they were to see her trying to

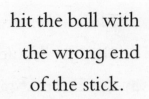

hit the ball with
the wrong end
of the stick.

'So, Erika,'
said Danny,
after a few
minutes of
the practice.
'You're doing
really well and
everything, but this is
a big match we've got coming
up, so perhaps you should come along to
the third-team practice on Tuesdays?'

'It's fine!' said Erika. 'I've decided
hockey's not really my thing. I'll just be
one of the ball girls – you know, like at
Wimbledon!'

'That's *tennis*,' said Danny.

'Oh, yeah,' replied Erika, grinning. 'I guess I'll just watch then.'

'Okaaaay,' said Danny, looking sideways at her. 'If you like.'

At every opportunity throughout the school day, Erika trailed Danny like an enthusiastic and very talkative shadow. Surely there would be *something* that stood out as being upsetting or troubling? Something that was causing a problem and disturbing his dreams? Perhaps some of his friends were being secretly unkind to him? Maybe there was a teacher giving him a hard time? It could be that he had a secret fear of carpets or door handles . . .

But no. Danny was absolutely fine

walking across carpet and operated many door handles throughout the day. It was baffling. He was exactly as he'd always seemed to be – totally confident, happy and calm.

The school bell rang for the end of the day and Erika waited by the gates, watching everyone file out, swinging their bags round, or dragging them across the floor and then getting told off by their parents. In among that throng of school life she saw Danny, smiling and laughing with a friend.

Whatever was going on with him, it wasn't to do with school. Erika frowned. If it wasn't to do with school, what *was* it?

There was only one way to find out.

'Hey, Danny!' called Erika, running up behind him. 'Fancy coming round to mine?'

'Er.' Danny's eyes widened. 'Well, I mean – I guess I could, but—'

'Great!' said Erika, punching him lightly on the arm. 'Except, actually, my house is being redecorated, so we'll have to go to yours instead.'

This was true. Or at least, partly true. Her dad had spent an unhappy weekend painting the living room last summer, and there was still the bit around the doorframes to do. So technically, it was still being decorated.

'We'll have to go to *mine*?' said Danny, raising one eyebrow.

'If you insist!' replied Erika. 'This is going to be **FUN!'**

Danny looked at Erika and shrugged weakly.

CHAPTER 6

Erika and Danny were walking along a broad, tree-lined street. Erika whistled slowly under her breath as she looked around.

'Wow! Just look at these houses,' she said, then nodded towards a particularly huge and impressive property across the road. 'Imagine living somewhere like that!'

'Er, I do live there,' replied Danny, turning into the driveway, and walking past an expensive-looking car.

'*Oh*,' said Erika, 'wow . . .'

'Hey, Dad!' called Danny as he opened the front door. 'I've brought a friend back from school – is that OK?'

'Yeah, of course!' replied Danny's dad, coming down the stairs. 'Hello,' he said, smiling at Erika. 'I don't think we've met?'

'This is Erika,' said Danny. 'She's, uh, a new friend?' He sounded slightly unsure.

'Nice to meet you, Mr Forsyth!' said Erika, smiling broadly.

'Nice to meet you too, Erika,' said Danny's dad. 'So, do you know Danny from cricket club?'

'Er, no,' said Erika.

Danny's dad peered at her. 'Debating club?'

'No,' said Erika, 'although Danny did suggest that I join!'

'Did I?' asked Danny. 'I don't remember that.' He frowned, and his eyes narrowed. 'Or *do* I? Something about it sounds kind of familiar . . .'

Erika bit her lip. Of course he didn't remember – he'd said that in the dream last night. 'The thing is, I don't know Danny from *any* clubs,' Erika said quickly. 'I don't really do any clubs. No, Danny and I are just friends because we both like —' she paused for a moment, racking her brains — '*cheese*?'

'I thought you hated cheese!' said Danny's dad, turning to look at his son.

'I *do*!' insisted Danny. 'Always have, always will!'

'OK,' said Danny's dad slowly. 'Well, I've got some work to finish off — there are snacks in the fridge.'

'Great, thanks! See you later, Dad,' said Danny. He turned to Erika. 'So, fancy a snack?' He slowly raised one eyebrow. 'Maybe a big slab of cheese?'

'Ha!' Erika grinned as they walked

through to the kitchen. 'Yeah, I'm not quite sure where that came from. Anyway, your dad seems nice.'

'Yeah.' Danny's face lit up. 'I know lots of people moan about their parents, but both mine are great. They're kind of like my friends as well, you know?'

Erika sighed. It wasn't that she wanted Danny to have a difficult home life, but she did want to find a clue about what was upsetting his dreams. 'Can they be a bit pushy though? You know, forcing you to sign up to loads of clubs and stuff?'

Danny looked at her. 'No, nothing like that!' he said. 'If anything, they want me to take less stuff on! Mum keeps chatting about "self-care". You know, taking the time to *just be*.'

'Your mum sounds sensible!' said Erika.

Danny shrugged. 'I guess I just like to keep busy.'

'But why?' asked Erika, her eyes narrowing. 'Why's it so important to keep busy?' She scratched her chin. 'If it's not school and it's not your home life, *what is it*?'

'What's what?' asked Danny.

'Er, what is it that . . .' Erika wracked her brains for something to complete the sentence (hopefully it would be nothing to do with cheese this time). 'What it is that makes you so –' she paused, then her face broke out into a relieved smile – 'so *good* at everything!'

Danny looked at her. 'You want to know my *amaaaaaaaaazing* secret?' He waggled his fingers through the air like a magician. Erika grinned. 'It's kind of boring, actually,' Danny continued. 'It's just practice.'

'But why do you want to be good at everything?' pressed Erika.

'I don't want to,' replied Danny evenly. 'I just like doing lots of things, and if you do something enough, you get good at it.'

Erika's eyebrows dipped together. This wasn't very helpful at all. She was sure that Danny was hiding something from her, or possibly even from himself . . .

Over the next hour, Danny showed Erika round his house, they played some games, and they bounced on his trampoline. Before long, she'd almost completely forgotten that she was there on official **DREAM DEFENDERS** business and was just having fun. It wasn't until it was time for her to go home that she realized she was still no closer to working out what that Nightmare was in his dreams. Everything about him seemed totally fine.

Erika frowned. That wasn't going to be very helpful for their mission that night.

CHAPTER 7

'That's all you've got?' growled Wade in the **DREAM DEFENDERS** briefing room later that night. 'You spend a whole day with him and all you can report is, "everything about him just seems totally fine".'

'I'm just telling you what I saw!' protested Erika. 'Anyway, what now? We still don't know what that monster is, *or* how to defeat it!'

'We *can't* defeat it,' said Madam Hettyforth firmly. 'All the **DREAM**

DEFENDERS can really do is help and support. At the end of the night, it's only the Dreamer who can fight their own Nightmare.'

Erika nodded. 'I know – it's just that you all have these *amazing* powers!'

'Not just us,' said Madam Hettyforth, her eyes bright. 'I see that your skills are coming on well too! Silas showed me the footage of you creating a staircase out of a cliff a few nights ago – impressive work!'

Erika flushed. 'Thank you! I've been practising a lot! I just wish we could do more to help. You know, make things easier for the Dreamers?'

Madam Hettyforth smiled kindly. 'I know,' she replied, 'but imagine how much harder it would be for the Dreamers to fight a Nightmare without our help.' She looked around at the **DREAM DEFENDERS** and clapped her hands briskly together. 'Now, come on! Buck up, everyone! You all need to get back in there, track that Nightmare, work out what's causing it and, ideally, help Danny to get rid of it!'

'Yes, Ma'am!' chorused the **DREAM DEFENDERS**.

One by one, they filed out of the door, heading towards the dream portals. Just as Erika was about to leave, Madam Hettyforth touched her arm.

'I know it's hard, Erika,' she said. 'You want to be able to fix everything, for everyone. But the trouble is that unless someone's been able to fix their own problem, it's not really fixed; it's just gone away for a bit. Does that make sense?'

'I think so,' replied Erika.

Madam Hettyforth smiled broadly. 'Now, you get out there and you help that boy. OK?'

Erika grinned. 'Will do, Ma'am!' She hurried off to catch up with the rest of the **DREAM DEFENDERS**.

'Everyone ready?' asked Sim, keying in the code to open the portal to Danny's dream. The **DREAM DEFENDERS** nodded. 'Right! Here we go then!' Sim pressed the final key. Dazzling light flared as the portal opened, and, one by one, they all stepped through.

* * * * *

'Where on earth are we?' asked Erika. 'And what's happening?' She gazed around with an expression that was equal parts amusement and total confusion.

A monumentally huge bone shone triumphantly on a hilltop nearby, and the air was filled with the words 'Walkies!' 'Dinner!' and 'Who's a good boy?' being repeated over and over again.

Something small and hard hit the side of Erika's head. It had just started raining, but it wasn't rain that was falling from the sky. Next to her, Beastling bent down and picked up a dog treat from the floor.

'Hmmm,' mused Silas, tapping on his electronic device. 'It looks like we've been separated from the others. It must be another problem with the systems. We're not anywhere near where we're meant to be. By the looks of it, we're not even in Danny's dream—'

He was interrupted as a horde of cats and squirrels suddenly ran past, all of them calling out, '*Chase me! Chase me!*'

Beastling scratched his head and muttered, '**Heebie Jeebie!**' creating an image of a sleeping dog with thought bubbles coming out of its head.

'Beastling's right!' exclaimed Silas. 'We must be inside a dog's dream!'

The landscape shifted and Erika, Silas and Beastling suddenly found themselves on the comfiest sofa EVER, positioned just in front of a lovely cosy fire. Erika felt an almost overwhelming urge to curl up and try to scratch her ear with her back leg.

She shook her head.

'Right! This is *too* weird! We need to get out of here, now! Any ideas how we find the others?'

'We'll have to dream surf,' replied Silas. 'We catch the psychic energy the next time the dream shifts and use it to ride into the nearest dream. Then we keep doing that until we find the others.'

'How long will that take?' asked Erika.

Silas shook his head. 'Hard to say for sure, but the next wave hits in twenty seconds, so get ready!'

'Get ready for what?' she demanded. 'What do we do?'

'When I say run,' explained Silas, 'you run! Fast. Got it?' He then grabbed Erika and Beastling by the hand and shouted, 'Run! Now!'

They all started sprinting forward, then Silas yelled, 'Now, *JUMP!*'

Erika jumped, the world folded up around her like an origami sculpture. With a dazzling flash of light, Erika, Beastling and Silas blinked out of existence.

CHAPTER 8

Wade and Sim were standing behind Danny, watching him trying to pack a small travel bag with a huge number of very large things while a countdown timer ticked away loudly in the background.

Wade was scribbling notes in a little pad when the air shimmered behind him and Silas, Erika and Beastling leaped forward through a rip in the fabric of the dream.

'You took your time!' exclaimed Wade. 'Trying to get out of all the hard work, were you?'

Erika, Silas and Beastling were soaking wet and covered in a mixture of feathers, mud and wire wool.

'Don't. Even. *Start!*' growled Erika. 'We've been in a fish dream, a cat dream, a worm dream and even a robot's dream, which was full of electronic sheep!'

'Well, you're here now!' said Sim, turning herself into a hosepipe and washing them thoroughly. Then she shapeshifted into a giant hairdryer. Seconds later, Erika, Silas and Beastling were all clean and dry, if a bit fluffy-looking. 'So, what's been happening while we were gone?' asked Silas.

Sim shrugged. 'We've stayed hidden while we tried a few things out.' She paused and shuffled her feet on the floor.

'What "things"?' asked Erika.

'Well,' said Sim slowly, 'we thought it *might* be some kind of Anxietymare that's bothering him.'

'It's a possibility,' said Silas, nodding. 'So what's the plan? How are you helping him relax and manage his anxiety?'

Sim didn't respond.

Wade sighed heavily. 'We've been trying to lure that Nightmare out into the open by trying to make Danny feel anxious and worried. If it's an Anxietymare, it'll come running!'

There was a pause. Then Erika said, 'Just to be clear, you think Danny might have anxiety, so you've been helping him by –' she shook her head – 'making him *anxious*?'

'And what would YOU suggest, Delgano!' growled Wade.

'Arguing's not going to help!' interrupted Sim. 'Besides, I don't think anything could make Danny anxious! Seriously, he's not worried about heights, confrontation, getting lost or eating beetroot!'

'Eating beetroot?' repeated Erika.

Sim shrugged. 'We had to try everything!'

Just then Danny muttered, 'Yessss!' under his breath. He'd somehow managed to pack everything into the tiny bag just as the timer went off.

'Seriously?' murmured Wade. 'He packed it *all* in? Even the motorbike and the hippo?'

'It's all in there,' said Sim. She turned back to Erika. 'I don't think there's anything that this kid can't do!'

Erika shook her head. 'OK, so in some ways, Wade's right – we do need to know what this thing is; I just don't like sneaking around to do it. So, let's use the F.A.B. again, OK?'

Wade glanced round at Silas and Sim, who both nodded. He pulled out the Full Awareness Blast and directed it towards Danny. A bright light flashed out of the device, and a moment later Danny was blinking heavily as he looked around.

'Wait,' he murmured, 'this is a dream! I knew it was weird to be trying to fit a rowing boat into a rucksack!'

'Hi, Danny!' called Erika brightly. 'Remember me?'

Danny smiled at Erika. 'Yeah, hi, Erika! But it's so strange – now I remember you from today *and* the dream last night.' He shook his head slowly. 'This is *so* strange!'

Erika grinned. 'That's dreams for you! Anyway, look, the bad news is that we're no closer to working out what that Nightmare is, or what it wants with you.'

Danny looked around wildly. 'What do you mean? What Nightmare? I can't see anything!'

'There's nothing there right now!' said Erika. 'But there was in the dream last night, and it's going to be here now too, *somewhere*. It's just a matter of time before it finds you, so we need to work out *what*

it is so we can help you get rid of it.'
She looked Danny straight in the eyes.
'Seriously, Danny, that thing is bad news,
so we're going to run a few tests, OK?'

Danny shrugged. 'I guess,' he said.

'Good lad!' interrupted Wade. 'I'll get
the medieval torture instruments.'

Danny's eyes widened.

'One thing you should know about
Wade,' said Erika, glaring at Wade
and putting her arm around Danny's
shoulders, 'is that he's *not at all* funny.'

'I dunno. I thought that was pretty
good,' chuckled Wade.

'I can't believe it!' said Erika, shaking her
head. 'Somehow, he can even run through

Nightmare treacle!' She glanced over at Silas. 'Have you ever seen that before?'

'Not often,' replied Silas, watching Danny jog lightly though the invisible – but incredibly thick – treacle that the Nightmares used as a trap. Ordinarily, the treacle would slow a Dreamer down, making it impossible for them to move quickly or fight back if they were under

attack, but not in Danny's case.

Sim looked round at the rest of the **DREAM DEFENDERS**. 'What now? It looks like *nothing* bothers him!'

'I know,' replied Erika, rubbing at her temples. She looked over at Danny. 'It's like you can do anything! I mean, it doesn't look like you need any help at all, and yet . . .' She paused. 'You must – otherwise we wouldn't be here.'

Danny looked at her. 'What if I was wrongly identified? You were saying you'd had lots of tech problems. Maybe I don't need your help?'

Beastling pulled a face and made a (very small) picture of a person showing off, but he made sure that Danny couldn't see it. That didn't matter though because no one was looking at him.

A hideous ripping sound had just torn through the air. At first Erika couldn't even tell what direction the sound was coming from – it seemed to be everywhere at once. A gnarled, taloned hand slashed through the fabric of the dream, and out leaped the flickering, shapeshifting monster. Erika gazed upwards, her eyes wide. If anything, it looked even bigger now as it towered above them, shrieking in wild fury.

CHAPTER 9

The **DREAM DEFENDERS** scattered. Sim, Erika and Beastling dragged Danny to safety, while Silas and Wade immediately began circling the monster.

'Looks like we've got another fight on our hands!' growled Wade. He glared up at the Nightmare, his hands clenched into fists. 'Come on then! Show us what you've got!'

'Wade!' shouted Silas. 'Can you distract it while I take some readings? We need to find out what we're dealing with here!'

Wade nodded. 'I'll try!' He swept his hands in a huge circle and immediately rocks, stones and pebbles started to detach themselves from the ground all around him. He closed his eyes and gritted his teeth, until the mass of stone melted into boiling hot lava. He flung it up towards the Nightmare.

The Nightmare flinched and hissed furiously as it raised its hands in front of its face to stop the lava.

'Ha!' shouted Wade. 'You don't like **THAT**, do you!'

But the smile vanished from his face as he realized that the monster had caught the lava, and was tossing it lightly from hand to hand. Then, with a twisted smile drawn across its face, it flung the cooling mass of lava and rock towards Erika and Danny.

Time seemed to slow down. Danny still couldn't see the Nightmare, but he could see the smouldering rocks hurtling towards them. His eyes widened as he looked at Erika.

'What—' he began, but just in the nick of time, Wade reached his hand out and seconds later the rock was a pile of tiny pebbles and dust, which fell harmlessly to the floor.

'Thanks!' Erika called out. Wade nodded back in return.

'Got anything, Silas?' yelled Sim.

Silas shook his head as he tapped at an electronic device and directed it towards the monster. 'Not yet – I need a bit longer!'

'OK, here goes!' said Sim. She morphed into a giant sea monster, towering up just as high as Danny's Nightmare.

'Try picking on someone your own size!' she bellowed as she lunged towards the creature. But as she got within striking distance, the monster shrank, changing shape and easily springing out of the way.

'Oh!' gasped Sim as she flew forward through the air where the monster had been standing just moments earlier.

Wade pressed his hands to the floor and the ground churned. Massive stones rose up, rumbling around as they heated up, this time forming a huge pool of lava underneath the Nightmare. It screamed furiously as it sank down into the boiling pool. Wade immediately cooled it all

down, turning the lava
back into rock and
trapping the creature
inside.

One smouldering clawed hand was all that was visible, protruding from the surface.

'Is it over?' asked Sim, morphing back into her usual form.

'For now,' replied Wade.

'Great work, Wade!' said Silas. 'It'll be easy to get an accurate reading now!'

'Look, what's going on?' shouted Danny. 'I can see lava flying around the place and you lot all dancing round, but why? I can't see *anything* there!'

'I've got an idea!' said Erika. 'Wade, have you got an In-Sight Visor?'

'Yes!' replied Wade, reaching inside the storage compartment in his chest. 'Great idea, Erika!' He pulled out a visor and tossed it over towards Erika, and then pulled out a big bag of doughnuts. 'I've got some doughnuts too. Anyone else fancy one?'

'Er, maybe later?' said Sim.

'Suit yourself.' Wade shrugged and popped four doughnuts in his mouth at once.

Erika placed the In-Sight Visor over Danny's head and turned it on. For a moment he just looked around, but when he saw the stone prison and the giant clawed hand, he gasped.

He flicked the visor up and blinked. 'With the visor on, I can totally see it! But as soon as I take it off, there's nothing! That's so strange!'

'It doesn't fix your problem, but it'll be a lot easier to avoid that Nightmare now you can see it,' replied Erika.

'It must be massive!' said Danny, staring up at the clawed hand that twitched and flexed above him.

'Yeah, it is,' replied Erika. 'See what we were so worried about now?'

Danny nodded silently, unable to drag his eyes away from the hideous hand. He stared at it, almost hypnotized.

For a moment everything was still, and then, without warning, the stone prison exploded. Shards of rock and dust shot into the air as the Nightmare rose up, bigger than ever.

'OK, I've got a full scan!' yelled Silas. 'Let's go analyse the data somewhere else; then we can work out how to defeat it—'

He was interrupted by a loud yell as Danny ran towards the Nightmare and flung a rock at it. The rock flew up high into the air, and then landed with a quiet thud near the foot of the monster. It squinted at the rock, and then back at Danny, and scratched its head.

'I'm not leaving till this thing's beaten!' shouted Danny.

'We need to know more about it!' said Erika, grabbing his arm. 'We can't just rush in there without knowing what we're facing. It's like Silas said – we need to get somewhere safe to work out what to do next.'

'Oh yeah?' replied Danny, his cheeks

flushed. 'Well, I've never run away from anything in my life!'

The Nightmare rose above them, huge and overwhelming.

'Think of this as a first then!' cried Erika. 'Silas? Can you teleport us out of here?'

Silas nodded. 'Yes, that's *probably* for the best!'

Erika and Beastling tried to heave Danny away from the Nightmare towards Silas, Wade and Sim,

who were running over. In the end they all made a chain, with Erika grabbing hold of Danny, and Beastling reaching out towards Silas. The Nightmare roared and bellowed, flailing arms, legs, tentacles, and other less-identifiable appendages around in the air. Silas began the teleportation and the familiar dizzying sensation rose up within Erika. She heard Danny yell something and twist round to hurl another rock towards the monster. The sudden movement made Beastling's hand slip away from Silas's mid-teleportation. With the chain broken, Erika, Beastling .

and Danny found themselves tumbling through space, completely alone.

CHAPTER 10

Erika, Danny and Beastling were spinning wildly out of control. They tumbled fast through the air, towards a ground gleaming with white sand dunes. Erika crashed hard, sprawled on the sand, and was soon followed by Danny, who landed on her leg, making her cry out in pain. Beastling slammed down a second later, rolling in a furry ball down the sand dune. For a moment they all just lay there, gasping for breath.

'What just happened?' groaned Danny.

'You just got us lost!' yelled Erika. 'You broke our connection with Silas mid-teleportation! We could be *anywhere* now!'

Danny glanced around. 'It looks like somewhere I went on holiday when I was little, but the sand dunes here go on for, well – for ever!'

'That's dreams for you,' muttered Erika, scowling as she climbed to her feet. 'Snippets of memory cut up and put back together in a different order.' She winced as she put weight on her right leg, and glared at Danny. '*And* you've hurt my leg!' she muttered, a familiar heat rising up within her. 'What were you *thinking*? You can't defeat a Nightmare by throwing *stones* at it!'

'Well, I had to do something, didn't

I!' shouted Danny. 'And what were *you* doing? It looked like you wanted to just run away!'

'We weren't *running away*!' yelled Erika. 'We were going to work out what to do!

To solve *any* problem, you need to know what it is! You don't just throw things at it and hope for the best!'

'Yeah? Well, I'm sorry that I'm not as *smart* as you, and—'

'**Heebie Jeebie!**' bellowed Beastling, in a surprisingly loud voice for such a small creature. A massive speech bubble appeared with two people furiously arguing and a big cross through it.

Beastling folded his arms and stared at Danny and Erika. His head was tilted to one side, and he looked very much like a teacher who's about to tell you that they're not angry with you, just very disappointed.

'Beastling's right,' said Erika, after a

moment. 'This won't get us anywhere. I'll contact the others and they can come and rescue us.' She pulled out an electronic device from her pocket, but the screen was smashed. A tangle of wires poked out of the broken casing.

'Or, perhaps I won't,' she added, shaking her head.

'Look, I'm sorry, all right?' said Danny.

'I guess it's just that I normally find a way to solve most problems by myself.' He paused and looked down at the ground.

'There's nothing wrong with getting a bit of help,' said Erika, looking directly at Danny. 'You like to help other people, right? Like the younger kids you teach football?'

Danny nodded. 'Sure, but they *need* the help, don't they?'

'And you don't?' pressed Erika, raising an eyebrow. 'You *never* need any help, with anything?'

'I'm not saying that!' Danny laughed. 'It's just . . .' He trailed off.

'It's just that is *exactly* what

you're saying?' suggested Erika.

'I dunno,' muttered Danny, shaking his head. 'But anyway, *that* doesn't matter right now. We need to find the others, don't we?'

'Yeah,' replied Erika. 'But I don't know where *we* are, or where *they* are. It's not going to be easy.'

Having a concrete problem to focus on seemed to cheer Danny up a bit. 'So, let's head for higher ground!' he said, looking around. 'We'll have a better view from up high.'

'Yeah, that's a good idea,' said Erika. 'I've also got an emergency flare. We can set that off and hopefully the others will spot it.'

'But won't it be better if *we* find them?'

said Danny. 'You know, it'll prove that we're not helpless! That we can solve our own problems!'

Erika narrowed her eyes. It was strange: that was exactly what Madam Hettyforth had said the Dreamers needed to do – solve their own problems. But surely not by doing something that would make it harder for them to succeed . . . She frowned. This whole dream was unlike any other she'd ever been in. Danny wasn't like one of their usual Dreamers – perhaps the usual rules didn't apply?

'Let's just leave the flare for a bit,' suggested Danny. 'We can give it our best shot, and then use it if we absolutely have to.'

Erika looked around. There was no

immediate danger in sight.

'OK,' she sighed. 'But at the first sign of trouble, this flare is going off. Got it?'

'Fair enough,' Danny said. Then he immediately started scrambling up towards the top of the gleaming sand

dune. 'Come on – I *bet* we'll be able to see them from up here!' He glanced back at Erika and Beastling, who were looking sceptically at each other, and grinned. 'Keep up!'

CHAPTER 11

Erika looked at the picture Beastling was making. It showed Danny trying to juggle, solve world hunger and jet-ski, all at the same time, all on his own.

She nodded. 'That's about it,' she replied, ruffling her small furry friend's ears. 'But why? Why does he feel that he's got to be able to do everything all on his own?'

Beastling shrugged.

'I guess that's what we need to find out,' added Erika as they scrambled up towards the top of the sand dune. Danny was already halfway up the next one.

'Hurry up!' Danny shouted, his voice sounding thin and distant.

'Well, you heard him!' said Erika to Beastling, and together they ran, jumped, and rolled down the side of the massive dune until they reached the bottom, and then started climbing up behind Danny. They were almost at the top when

Danny turned and started sprinting down the dune.

'Now what?' muttered Erika under her breath. But her question was answered by a huge roar. The dune underneath her feet started to quake, and sand poured down the slopes towards them.

The Nightmare rose over the peak of the dune, a huge monstrosity of a thing, making ear-splitting shrieks. Somehow, it seemed even bigger than before. Shockwaves tore beneath Erika as the ground vibrated with each explosive footfall.

Heart pounding in her chest, Erika spun around and sprinted down the dune.

Behind her the Nightmare reached down, burrowing its hand into the sand, a cruel smile spread across what passed for its face, as it flung a boulder towards Danny. He dived forward and the boulder shot over his head, landing with a *whumph* in the sand.

'Good job I'm captain of the dodgeball team!' Danny gasped as he caught up with Erika and Beastling.

'We're never going to make it like this!' yelled Erika as they ran. 'We need to move faster!' She stopped running for a moment and closed her eyes tight, pressing her hands together.

'What are you doing?' gasped Danny, as the monster got closer and closer. 'I thought you said we needed to move *faster*!'

'We do!' replied Erika. 'Give me a second.'

'Well, I'd give you whole *minutes*,' said Danny, 'but I'm not sure that our friend back there is going to! So, whatever you're doing, make it quick!'

'OK, it's ready!' cried Erika. The next moment a large bathtub appeared next to them. 'Hop in!'

'How did you do that!' said Danny, his jaw hanging open.

'I'll explain another time!' said Erika urgently. 'Just get in!' The Nightmare's breath was hot on her neck, her eardrums were buzzing from its incessant screaming.

Danny and Beastling jumped into the bath. Erika gave it a hard shove and then leaped in behind them. The bath quickly picked up speed and was soon shooting down the dune, a huge plume of sand spraying out behind it.

'What happens when we get to the bottom?' Danny called out, glancing nervously behind them. 'We can't sledge uphill!'

Erika just smiled as she closed her eyes again. She concentrated hard. Somehow, the world shifted, and the dune kept on going down.

'*What*?' gasped Danny. 'Did you just . . . *change the world*?'

Erika grinned. 'Maybe a little bit,' she replied. 'I'm still learning and I'm not as good as Silas or Wade, but so long as we can keep doing this, we should be able to stay ahead of that Nightmare!' She shot

a look over her shoulder and swallowed heavily. She closed her eyes once more and pressed her fingers against the side of her head, breathing out heavily. Seconds later, the slope increased in steepness and the bath gained even more speed. Erika twisted around, hoping to see the Nightmare fading into the distance, but it was no good. It was *still* gaining on them.

'OK, that's *it!*' she cried. 'I'm setting that flare off!' She reached into her pocket and pulled out the flare. In one action, she triggered it and flung it over her shoulder. For a moment the flare just followed the arc of Erika's throw, then it seemed to take on a life of its own and shot into the sky like a rocket. It flew upwards just as the

Nightmare
was lunging
down towards
them. For a
moment it looked
like it would collide
with the huge monster, but
the rocket seemed to pass straight
through, just making the creature
shimmer slightly as it went.

'Did you see that!' gasped Erika. But
Danny and Beastling had been focusing
on what was ahead of them.

Erika's mind was racing. What was
happening here? Why had the creature
shimmered? She leaned over the edge
of the speeding bath and scrutinized
the monster. Now that she was looking

closely, she noticed that occasionally it seemed to flicker and glitch in places, like a faulty video file. Were those mirrors beneath it? Lenses of some sort? It was hard to say with any certainty, but an idea started to form in her mind.

'Danny!' called Erika. 'Listen! What if that Nightmare's *not* massive? What if it just *looks* massive? You know how an angry cat makes its fur stand on end to appear bigger?'

Danny looked at her. 'So you're saying it's not real?'

'Not exactly,' replied Erika. 'Just different. Smaller. Less of a problem than it looks. If we can just work out what the problem really is, you might realize that it's not as big as it seems, and then the

Nightmare might shrink!'

Danny's eyes narrowed. 'If it's not *really* this big, why are we running away?' He turned around and climbed awkwardly over Erika towards the back of the bath. 'I'm going to finish this. Right now!' He leaped out, landing with a skid on the shifting sands of the dune.

'*No!*' yelled Erika as the bath sped away from Danny. 'That's *not* what I meant!'

CHAPTER 12

Erika leaped out of the bath, pulling Beastling with her. She landed unsteadily on the sand and then started sprinting up hill, but it was incredibly hard work. Erika squeezed her eyelids together,

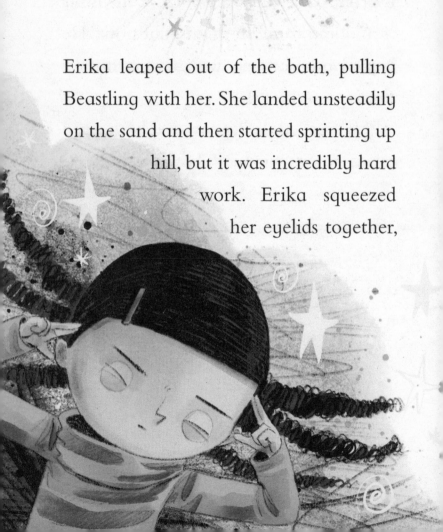

focusing on levelling off the landscape again. Slowly, the world tilted like an enormous see-saw, and moments later it was flat.

Erika took a deep breath. Her vision was blurred and her head was spinning. Beastling looked up at her, his eyebrows wrinkled in the middle.

'I'm fine,' she murmured, shaking her head to try to clear it. 'Come on, we need to get Danny to safety.'

In the distance, Danny was sprinting towards the creature, his hands balled into fists. He was yelling at the top of his voice.

'It's only small if you KNOW that it's small!' shouted Erika. 'Until you've worked out how to shrink your problem, that Nightmare is still *very* big, and *VERY* dangerous!'

But Danny ignored her. He was still running towards the monster, his face twisted up in anger while the monster just laughed a cruel, shrieking sound.

Erika tried to change the landscape again, to create a hole beneath the Nightmare, but she was too slow. By the time the hole had formed, the monster had leaped out of the way.

Erika watched in horror. Why wouldn't Danny listen to her? She was only trying to help.

Danny sprinted through the creature's legs. It bent down malevolently to try to grab him, but he rolled out of the way and weaved back around, making the monster twist and reach for him again. Somehow, Danny managed to avoid the massive hand as it scrabbled around.

'He's trying to make it dizzy!' exclaimed Erika. 'And it looks like it *might* work! Come on, Beastling – let's help!'

Feet slipping on the soft sand, Erika and Beastling ran forward, just as Danny skidded under the Nightmare's legs once more. He took aim and hurled a rock up towards it. But the rock simply sailed through the creature and fell back towards him, crashing on to his leg. Danny cried out in pain and tried to stand, but he fell to his knees, teeth gritted together. The monster grinned, circling back around to Danny, its small eyes lighting up. It was ready to feed.

Erika closed her eyes once more. She imagined the sand dune forming a tunnel right beneath Danny, a chute that slid down and away from the monster. The sand started to morph, forming the steep tunnel, just as Erika had imagined it, and Danny slid away to safety, crying out in surprise and frustration.

Erika stumbled forward, weakened by all the energy she'd been expending. She tried to stand, to run, but her legs felt like jelly. The Nightmare reared up above her and Beastling in fury. Its mouth was an awful, cruel slash of sharp teeth and malice as it swept a huge clawed hand down towards them.

There was no time to do anything. Erika gasped; this was *it*. She winced as she reached out her hand towards Beastling. At least they would be together. She shut her eyes, teeth clenched, waiting for a sudden burst of unbearable pain.

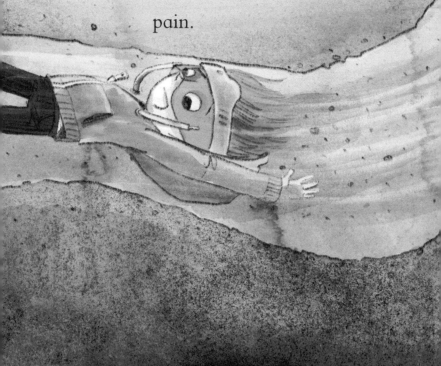

But it didn't come. Erika peered out through one narrowed eyelid.

The monster's face was shot through with surprise, its eyes wide as it slowed down and finally froze in place, claws just millimetres away from Erika's face. Only its eyes were moving.

Rising through the air behind the monster, sitting on a floating cloud, was Silas. In his hand was a large remote control. He was pointing it at the Nightmare, his finger firmly pressed on the pause button.

'I *love* this thing!' he said with a grin.

Then he leaped off the cloud and ran over to Erika. 'We saw the flare,' he added. 'Are you OK?'

'Better now you're here!' replied Erika. 'Look, we need to get some sense into Danny. He thinks he can take this Nightmare down all by himself, just by fighting with it!'

Silas frowned. 'OK, give me a second.' He pressed the rewind button on the remote and the Nightmare slowly started moving backwards. Its eyes flashed angrily as it moved against its will, quicker and quicker, repeating all of the movements it had just made in reverse, until it was lumbering away backwards over the sand dunes.

'That'll buy us a bit of time,' said Silas, 'but not much. A Nightmare this powerful isn't going to be controlled like that for long. But – wait, where *is* Danny?'

Erika pointed to the bottom of the long, curling chute she'd created. Danny was sat down, clutching his knee and wincing. Silas, Erika and Beastling skidded down the chute.

'So, is that it?' asked Danny quietly. 'Did you beat it?'

Silas shook his head. 'No, I was just able to send it away for a while. Is your leg OK?'

Danny breathed in sharply though his teeth. 'Looks like I'll be off the school sports teams for a while!'

'Don't worry about that,' said Erika. 'It's not your *real* leg; you'll be fine when you wake up. And Sim can probably get this fixed up when she gets here – she's good at that sort of thing. Can you stand?'

With Silas's help, Danny managed to get himself upright and was able to slowly limp forward a few steps.

'That was all my fault,' he said quietly, glancing at Erika then looking down at his feet. 'If Silas hadn't turned up, you could have been hurt. Badly.'

Erika shrugged. 'But he did, and I wasn't, so it's all OK.'

Danny shook his head. 'But it's not. I don't mind putting myself in danger, but I nearly got you hurt, or worse!' He screwed his face up and looked away.

'I just wanted to be able to fix it. You know? To make things better.'

'But you don't have to!' exclaimed Erika. 'Not all by yourself. We all need help sometimes, even the Amazing Danny Forsyth!'

'Yeah, but I don't want to be a problem, you know? I want to *fix* problems!' replied Danny. 'Other people have got a lot more stuff going on than me.'

'Perhaps,' replied Erika, 'but that doesn't mean that what you've got to cope with doesn't matter – that *you* don't matter!' She patted Danny on the arm. 'You've got to let us help you; you're not super-human after all! If we can work out what this Nightmare is after, then we stand a chance of beating it! So, can you do that? Can you at least *try* to let us help?'

Erika was smiling at Danny, Silas patted him on the back, and even Beastling made a picture bubble of an out-stretched hand being offered in support.

Danny took a deep breath, then nodded. 'I'll try,' he said.

CHAPTER 13

'*There* you are!' called Sim as she skidded over the top of a sand dune with Wade. 'We just saw our Nightmare friend stomping backwards away from here and followed the tracks.' She looked over at Danny, who was still clutching his leg. 'Everything OK?'

Danny shook his head. 'Not really.' He opened his mouth, as if to say something else, then shut it again.

'Is it your leg?' Sim prompted.

Danny looked at her for a moment. 'Well, yeah, but it's not just that . . .' He paused for a moment, then nodded, as if making his mind up about something. 'There's something I should have told you.'

Erika looked at him and smiled, her eyebrows lifting. 'Go on,' she said.

'So yeah, well, my mum and dad are kind of splitting up . . .' he said, blinking rapidly as his eyes grew shiny. 'I mean, compared to lots of other things in the world, it's not all that big a deal, but—'

'It's a big deal for you, Danny,' said

Erika, pulling him into a hug. 'It's *massive!*' Wade, Silas and Sim all nodded, and Beastling patted him on the leg.

'I just don't want to be a problem,' added Danny, looking around at everyone. 'I know that it's not been easy for my parents. They think I'm asleep when they talk about this stuff, but they've both been so upset.' He wiped away a tear. 'I didn't want to make things harder for them, so I just kind of pretended that I was fine with it all. Like it didn't bother me . . .' He paused again. 'But it *does*. It does bother me.'

'Of course it does!' said Erika. 'How come you never said anything before?'

Danny shrugged. 'I guess I felt I needed to work my own way through it. But instead of doing that, I pretended that it wasn't really happening. You know, I took on more and more things. I filled up *all* my time so I never had a chance to think about anything, or to work out how I was feeling.' He wiped his eyes. 'I should have told you earlier. I'm sorry.'

'It's fine, Danny,' said Erika. 'Look, we all deal with things differently, OK? But you're not alone! Lots of other people know what that feels like. Have you told anyone?'

Danny shook his head. 'I didn't want to bother anyone.'

'But it's *not* bothering them!' said Erika. 'That's life, isn't it? It's not all about winning football matches and things working out perfectly. Sometimes life's hard; sometimes it's sad; sometimes it just makes you *really* angry! But it's all *life*. It's *all* important! If you can let people into the bad bits, then the good parts you share with them mean even more! OK?'

Danny nodded as he looked at her.

'I am always here to listen,' added Erika. 'Whenever you want! And you know Kris, my friend from school?'

Danny nodded again, and Erika continued. 'Well, his parents split up last year, so he knows exactly what it feels like. You could always chat with him about it if you like?'

'Yeah, I think I'd like that,' said Danny. 'Thanks, Erika.'

'I hate to spoil the moment,' interrupted Wade, looking out towards the horizon through some binoculars, 'but that Nightmare's coming back. I'd say we've got about a minute!'

'We'll be ready for it this time,' said Erika firmly. 'We can all stand up to it. Together. Right, Danny?'

'Right,' replied Danny. 'Together.'

'Let me take a look at that leg of yours first,' said Sim. She knelt down and placed her hands either side of Danny's leg. She closed her eyes for a moment and then smiled. 'How's that?'

'It's . . .' Danny grinned at her as he placed his full weight on his leg. 'It feels fine! How did you do that?'

'We could discuss the complex links between the brain and nerve endings,' said Sim, 'and how your leg was never really injured because this is all just a dream, but that would get very long and complicated, so for now let's just say . . . *magic*!'

'Magic works for me!' replied Danny, grinning.

'What's the plan then?' asked Silas. His eyes were on the approaching Nightmare.

'I say we keep that thing busy and away

from Danny so that he gets a chance to look closely at it and see if he can find a way to break it down,' suggested Erika. 'Beastling and I will stick with him, and you lot give it hell, OK?'

'Sounds good to me,' growled Wade, pounding his stone fists together. 'I'm in the mood for a bit of *hell-giving*!'

'Then let's **DO IT!**' yelled Erika.

In a flurry of motion, the **DREAM DEFENDERS** all split off in different directions. Danny, Erika and Beastling headed up a dune to get a better vantage point. Silas dashed round the monster so fast he was a blur, leaving a trail of dazzling bright light behind him. The monster covered its eyes with one massive tentacle and hissed in confusion, taking a step backwards.

Wade thundered in, dragging up huge boulders right behind the Nightmare's feet. Sim morphed into a giant rhino and charged, thrusting the creature backwards so it tripped over the boulders and fell heavily to the floor.

'That's exactly what I was trying to do!' said Danny.

'I know!' replied Erika. 'And you totally had the right idea – there were just approximately two less of you than there needed to be!'

'I tried to take on a bit too much, didn't I?' said Danny.

Erika grinned. 'Well, now that you put it like *that* . . .'

'Wait!' Danny cried. 'I think I can see

something!' He squinted at the creature. 'Yes! I can see it now! You're right – it's like a projection! It just *looks* bigger than it actually is!' He blinked and then laughed. 'There's like, all these lenses and projectors making it seem huge, but it's actually kind of tiny underneath all of that.'

As he spoke, the Nightmare shimmered and glitched. For a moment, the lenses were clear to see.

'If we can shut off that projection, I think we'll have a chance!' said Danny. 'Can you keep distracting it while I sneak up behind it and turn it off?'

'Yeah, I think I've got an idea how we can do that!' said Erika. 'Let's go, Beastling!'

Erika and Beastling skidded down the hill, joining the battle just as Wade was making scores of huge boulders rise from deep within the dunes, spinning high up in the air before they rained down on the Nightmare. It roared as it frantically beat them away.

One by one, Erika relayed the plan to the other members of the **DREAM DEFENDERS**. Silas nodded and shot around the monster once more, leaving a blurring trail of light that made it dizzy. Sim morphed into a giant flying toaster with a single unicorn horn, leaving behind her own rainbow trail as she flew in circles around the Nightmare. Wade pressed his hands to the floor and made the dunes bind together into huge sandstone pillars, which tripped and slowed down the creature as it chased after them.

Erika ran right in front of the Nightmare, ignoring the shouts of concern from Wade and Silas. She slipped and fell, crying out loud, causing the monster to turn its blank eyes on her. It licked its lips. Then, letting out a terrifying, shrieking roar and shaking two huge fists in the air, the Nightmare rose up above her.

'*This had better work . . .*' muttered Erika, bracing herself. Sweat trickled down her brow as Danny crept round the back of the creature. He peered at the monster, frowning in concentration.

'*Come on . . .*' whispered Erika. 'You can do it – *I hope*!'

The monster tensed, clearly preparing to attack, when a smile suddenly broke out on Danny's face. He dived forward and out of sight.

With a jerking spasm and a harsh buzzing sound, the creature twitched and flickered, and then froze. Then, just like a balloon with all the air let out of it, the monster started to shrink, quickly getting smaller and smaller. As the Nightmare shrank, it revealed a complex framework of metal limbs and projectors, which had created its massive bulk. The huge metal skeleton ground to a halt, and there, standing in the middle of it, was the Nightmare, not much taller than Beastling.

It was suddenly a lot less intimidating.

It tried to roar in fury, but the sound that came out was so much smaller now – more like an angry cat. Beastling rushed forward with a net and swiped it over the top of the Nightmare, trapping it in place.

'Is that really what it was all along?' whispered Danny. He was holding a handful of power cables that he'd yanked out of the machine. 'It's *tiny*!'

'Most problems *seem* bigger than they really are,' said Erika, grinning.

'That's how they win,' added Silas. 'It doesn't matter if it's a Fearmare or an Angermare – whatever form they take, Nightmares always try to make you think you can't beat them, when there's usually a simple solution.'

'But it's all so obvious now!' said Danny.

There was a shimmering fizz and suddenly Beastling's net was empty.

'*What?* Where did it go?' cried Danny.

'Back to the Nightmare Zone,' replied Wade. 'It's not your problem any more. Of course, it'll find its way back into someone else's dream one day, but now we know its little tricks, it won't be such a big problem next time. So thanks for your help, Danny.'

'Thanks for *my* help?' Danny laughed.

'No way – thanks for *yours*!'

'Looks like we're all wrapped up here!' said Erika happily. There was a ping on her communication device and she peered down at her wrist. '**REBOOTING DREAMSCAPE?**' she said. 'What does *that* mean?'

'It means they can't fix all the problems we've been having recently,' replied Silas, who was reading the message from his own communication device. 'So they're going to do it the old-fashioned way.'

'They're going to turn the whole Dreamscape off and then on again?' asked Erika. 'Is that even possible?'

'Oh sure!' replied Sim. 'It happens more often than you'd think. Haven't you ever woken up in the middle of the night for no reason at all?'

'Right . . .' said Erika. 'So what happens to *me* when they reboot?'

'Nothing bad,' replied Silas. 'You'll just wake up back in your own bed.'

Silas scrolled down through the message, his eyes narrowing as he skimmed the details. 'And it's going to happen in approximately . . .' He paused. 'Oh, wow! Pretty much immediately!'

'But I didn't get a chance to say—' But even as Erika was speaking, the Dreamscape melted away and she ended up murmuring the word 'goodbye' as she woke up in her own bed, looking blearily around her room in the first light of a brand-new day.

CHAPTER 14

'Seriously. What's going on with you?' asked Kris as he and Erika walked into the school canteen later that morning. 'I mean, trying to join the *hockey* team? Just . . . *what?*'

Erika shrugged. 'Just because I've never played hockey before doesn't mean I can't start now,' she said. 'Although, to be honest, hockey's still not really my thing. Wait, there's Danny!' She waved and shouted, '*Hey, Danny!*'

'Danny Forsyth?' whispered Kris,

grabbing Erika's arm, his eyes wide. 'You're calling him over here?'

'Looks like it,' said Erika with a grin.

Danny smiled and waved enthusiastically. Then he paused, his face crumpling up in thought, before walking towards them.

'How come you two are friends?' hissed Kris.

Erika shrugged. 'The same reason you and me are,' she replied. 'Because we get on.'

'Hi, Erika,' said Danny as he caught up with them. 'And it's Kris, right?'

Kris nodded silently, his mouth hanging open.

'I had the weirdest dream last night,' said Danny, tapping Erika on the arm, 'and I think *you* were in it.'

'Me?' laughed Erika. 'How strange! What was it about?'

Danny shook his head. 'I can't remember – it's like . . . you know when a word is on the tip of your tongue? It's like that, but this is a thought on the tip of my *brain*!' He looked closely at Erika. 'I feel like I've seen you recently – like, *really* recently.'

'Well, I did come round to your house last night,' said Erika, grinning. 'That's pretty recent, isn't it?'

'I guess,' said Danny shaking his head.

'So, do you want to have lunch with us?' asked Erika. 'If you've not got a club or anything?'

'That'd be good,' replied Danny as they walked over to a clear table. 'And no clubs for me today. I've cut down on all that. It was feeling a bit much, you know?'

'Yeah, you're not super-human after all!' said Erika.

Danny smiled, but then a flicker of doubt passed over his face. 'Weird, do you ever get déjà vu? I could have sworn you've said those exact words before, but not here — somewhere . . . different . . .' His voice trailed off.

'You know what, Danny — you're not quite how I thought you'd be,' said Kris. 'I always thought you were like a robot, you know? Almost *too* perfect! But you're just like me and Erika – a bit weird!' He paused, his eyes widening as he realized what he'd just said. 'Er, no offence!'

Danny grinned. 'None taken,' he said.

'Don't mind Kris,' added Erika. 'It's like he's got a tap between his brain and his mouth that's always turned on full!'

'It's fine!' replied Danny. 'You know, it's actually refreshing to just say how you feel, isn't it?' He shook his head. 'It's like I never used to actually talk about how I felt – as if nobody got to see the *real* me? You must think that sounds pretty strange!'

'I know exactly what you mean,' said Erika.

Danny smiled, then looked down at the table. 'It's just, things have felt different since I found out my parents are splitting up.'

'Hey, I'm sorry,' said Kris, catching Danny's eye. 'I know exactly what that's like – my parents split up last year.'

'Yeah, I'd heard about that,' said Danny. 'Are you OK?'

'Pretty much,' said Kris. 'But I won't lie, it can be tough, *really* tough sometimes. The whole thing just feels so odd, you know? You're used to all being together and then . . . well, then you're not.' He sighed. 'But it *does* get easier, eventually. Life never goes back to how it was before, but it does get good again.'

'It does?' asked Danny, looking away and wiping his eyes with the back of his hand.

'Sure,' replied Kris. 'You'll see soon enough. And look, any time you want to chat about it, you come find me, OK? You don't need to go through this alone.'

'Thanks, Kris,' said Danny. 'That's what I'm just starting to realize. Hey, I know! Why don't you both come round to mine after school?'

'Yeah!' said Kris. 'How about it, Erika?'

Erika grinned. 'Absolutely! I've just got something to do first, so I'll call round when I'm finished, OK?'

'Sounds good!' said Danny. 'You know, I've not told anyone else about my parents yet.' He paused, frowning. 'At least, I don't think I have . . .' He trailed off again. 'Either way, just saying it out loud makes me feel loads better. So, thanks, you two!'

'That's what friends are for!' said Erika. 'Anyway, come on, let's get some food – I'm starving!'

After school, Erika waited until everyone had left and then walked out of the gate. The road was deserted, but even so, she took out a toy mobile phone from her pocket – talking to yourself makes much more sense if you're holding a phone, after all. Then she squeezed the magic crystal that hung from her necklace three times and waited for a response from **DREAM DEFENDERS HQ**. It wasn't long before she heard Madam Hettyforth's voice inside her head.

'Erika!' rang out the cut-glass tones of their unit commander. 'Fantastic work last night. Truly exceptional. It was a difficult case, and no mistake. To enable someone to solve their own problems by making them see that sometimes we all need to ask for help! Just brilliant. I'm not sure I'd have been able to solve that one when I was a field agent.'

'Come off it, Ma'am!' Erika laughed. 'There's not a Dreamscape problem that you couldn't solve!'

'Just take the compliment, Erika,' rumbled Wade's deep voice. 'Ma'am's right – you did really well.' He paused and then added, with a slight hint of jealousy, '*Again.*'

'And the good news is that the reboot worked!' chipped in Sim. 'Everything's back up and running now, no more problems!'

'So, we'll be seeing you in a few hours,' added Silas. 'Is there anyone nearby?'

Erika glanced around, but the street was still empty. 'No,' she replied, 'all clear.'

'Great, I'm switching to visuals then,' said Silas. 'Beastling wanted to say something.'

Erika pulled out the crystal and a projection beamed out of it, showing the inside of the **DREAM DEFENDERS HQ**. The whole team were stood in a circle, smiling at Erika. Beastling was in the centre, jumping up and down, his

face bright and his eyes shining.

'**Heebie Jeebie!**' he called out, and a speech bubble popped up showing a picture of Beastling looking at Erika through a magnifying glass, and a timer in the background counting down to zero.

'Ooh, that's a tricky one,' murmured Erika, scratching her forehead. 'No, wait! I've got it! *See you soon?*'

Beastling's beaming face smiled even more, and everyone laughed as he hopped up and down, grinning and nodding.

'Well, see you soon too, buddy!' she replied. 'I'd better get going now. I hope that you've got a good mission lined up for tonight?'

'Isn't it *always* a good mission?' asked Silas, grinning.

'I guess so!' replied Erika. She waved goodbye and tucked the crystal necklace back under her jumper.

Erika smiled as she walked towards Danny's house. Warm, pink sunlight shone between the trees that lined the road, fanning out shadows across the

pavement, contrasting strips of light and shade. Erika looked at the pattern. It seemed to echo everything in her life: day and night, happiness and sadness, success and failure – you could never really understand one without the other.

'Got to take the rough with the smooth,' Erika muttered to herself, grinning as she turned into Danny's driveway.

Danny and Kris came running round the side of the house, laughing, and Erika ran over to join them. Life was good. She had a few friends who really understood her and, on top of that, a secret nightlife as a member of the **DREAM DEFENDERS**.

Really, what more could anyone ask for?

TOM PERCIVAL

They're on a mission to banish the worries!

Chanda
AND THE
Devious Doubt

A fantastic **DREAM DEFENDERS**

TOM PERCIVAL

'I would have loved this book as a child' Marcus Rashford MBE

MARCUS RASHFORD BOOKCLUB CHOICE

Silas
AND THE
Marvellous Misfits

A fantastic **DREAM DEFENDERS** adventure!

ACKNOWLEDGEMENTS

I counted up all the books I'd made the other day and it came to twenty-five. Twenty-five currently published books, and a few more that are currently in production – Phew – I'm sure you'll agree, that's a lot of books by anyone's reckoning! Now, you might think that SOME authors would be struggling after twenty-five books to come up with ideas for who to mention in their acknowledgements sections, but not me! Oh no! The only problem that I have with coming up with the acknowledgements page is remembering how to spell 'acknowledgements' because it's a bit of a tricky word. Still, luckily I can just type 'AKNOLYGMENT' or something like that and my computer will shake its head wearily and correct my terrible attempt to the proper spelling.

So yeah, I guess my computer deserves an acknowledgement. Hmm, actually, I wonder if that's a first? Has anyone else ever acknowledged their computer? I'm not sure . . . If I was feeling inclined/could be bothered, then I'd look it up but I'm actually a bit behind on some deadlines, and frankly that would be a waste of my time.

Anyway, the good news is that this acknowledgements page is one of the three deadlines that I need to meet today. So as soon as I've finished it I can tick it off nice and neatly on my to-do list, and that will feel good, I mean I also have to do some paperwork and a bunch of washing up, and the grass is getting kind of long in the garden and could do with a mow before it gets totally out of control, but this probably isn't the time or place to list every chore I have to do. ALTHOUGH . . . I could also acknowledge our robot vacuum cleaner, because that tireless little fellow saves me a good few hours over the course of the year which I can put towards writing books and drawing pictures and stuff like that, so yeah, those are the two people/beings/things that I want to acknowledge here, my computer and my robot vacuum cleaner.

Thanks you guys, I couldn't have done it without you!

T. P.

June 2022

ABOUT THE AUTHOR

Tom Percival writes and illustrates all sorts of children's books. He has produced cover illustrations for the Skulduggery Pleasant series, written and illustrated the Little Legends series, the Dream Defenders series, as well as twelve picture books. His Big Bright Feelings picture book series includes the Kate Greenaway-nominated *Ruby's Worry*, as well as *Perfectly Norman* and *Ravi's Roar*. *The Invisible* is a powerful picture book exploring poverty and those who are overlooked in our society. In 2020 he created the animation *Goodbye Rainclouds*, for BBC Children in Need to celebrate unsung heroes and launch their campaign. He lives in Gloucestershire with his partner and their two children.